AF230823

You Were Mine For A Time

Four Hot, Steamy short stories

to tempt your senses.

Katie Santee

CONTENTS

ACKNOWLEDGEMENTS

There are so many people who have contributed in the making of this book and my career but there are a few whom I would like to specifically acknowledge.

First and foremost is Kisha Griffiths. Without her encouragement and belief in my abilities, I never would have attempted to write my first story. She has been a constant force behind each story I have written and without her friendship and advise I would be lost.

Sexy Fantasy Club gave me the opportunity to write for them, thus opening other doors in this amazing industry. Thank you so much for all you did for me.

My best friends Bonnie Royce and Joan Jarrell have been with me at my best and worst for over 40 years. Where would I be now if these two hadn't kept me out of trouble? I love you both so much. Thanks for always keeping my head above water.

To all of those who proofread my work, gave me your feedback and encouraged me to put this book together, I thank you. Most of all to a special person who believes in how I think and how I write. He opened a passion in me that I could put into written word and I will always love him till I leave this world.

Mostly to my family and especially my husband Steve who has stood by my side and put up with the hours of my being at my computer. When an idea hits me out of the blue, he sees it in my eyes and says to go write it down. Hours later he comes in to check on me, after he's fixed his own dinner. I love you so much....thank you for giving me my dream.

This book.

HOT STUFF

Taking the bus on a long-distance trip can be a real hassle. Here I am, going from Charleston, SC, to Fresno, CA., and the bus is full. Hot, sweaty people squished into rows of three seats on each side of the aisle. Yuk, this was going to be a bad trip. At least we weren't going to stop in every little dinky town along the way. This bus went farther between stops. So, I put the seat back, closed my eyes and settled in for the nightmare. The two ladies beside me did the same thing. A few hours later the bus slowed and pulled into Savannah, GA. It was right around supper time, so the driver gave us one hour to get something to eat and be back in our seats ready to leave.

When I got back to my seat, there was a gorgeous man sitting in the seat by the window. Guessing that he was in his thirties, he had dark brown hair, hazel eyes, wore a green pull-over shirt and jeans. He had sneakers on his feet. As I took my seat he looked over, said hello and turned to look back out the window. He seemed to be looking intently at or for something or someone, so I followed his gaze. Standing near the bus was a beautiful, slim blonde and she was waving at him and was signaling something to him. He nodded his head like he understood her and smiled broadly at her. Hum, just my luck. He had a girlfriend. Not just a handsome man, but I mean all out gorgeous and not available. Ugh...oh damn!! Then he looked away from the window and turned in his seat and looked right at me. Oh God. Now what do I say.

"Um, hi, my name is Dixie."

"Hi, I'm Ricky. Nice to meet you. You are very pretty." He then took my hand and held it to his lips and kissed it gently and let it go.

My face must have turned ten shades of red because he said, "I'm sorry if I embarrassed you. But you are. You have the sexiest green eyes and the most luscious red hair." He reached up to touch my hair as my hand knocked it away.

"How dare you try to flirt with me after you just said goodbye to your girlfriend!"

I was completely offended by this time. The look on his face went from puzzled to humorous in the blink of an eye. His smile grew bigger and his eyes brightened.

"Wow!!! We just met and already you're jealous! I'm flattered."

"Well, don't be. I'm not jealous. I don't even know you. It's just that one minute you are waving and smiling at the blonde on the platform and now you're flirting with me. I don't get it. Nor do I like it very much. It's not very flattering for either of us, meaning her nor I." I stated flatly.

Again, Ricky's smile covered his face and I wanted so badly to reach up and slap it off.

"What the hell is so damn funny?" I asked.

"You are jealous. You wouldn't be acting like this if you weren't."

"You sir, are so full of yourself." I started to turn away from him, but he stood up and took a hold of my arms. He stood so tall that he had to duck his head to keep from hitting the ceiling of the bus. He sat me down in my seat and then returned to his own seat, turning to look straight into my eyes.

"Look Dixie, if you weren't paying attention to something that wasn't your business, you wouldn't be acting like a jealous schoolgirl. But I will let your jealous self-know that the woman on that platform is my sister, not my girlfriend. We were saying goodbye because I won't be seeing her for the next few years.

She is going away to college in Massachusetts next week for medical school. And, I will be clear across the country with my law practice. So, miss know it all. Are you satisfied?" With that, he turned and looked out the window as the bus pulled out of the terminal.

I sat there starring at my hands that were sitting in my lap. I had no idea what to say. Stupid didn't even begin to describe how I was feeling at the moment. We sat there in silence for a couple of hours. The lady sitting to my left was sound asleep within a half hour of us being on the road. This was really going to be a shitty trip. I pushed my backrest back and closed my eyes.

Ricky was reading a book...probably some law stuff. And I had already made enough of an ass of myself...so I chose to remain quiet.

Soon, with the rumble of the road, I was sound asleep. At some point I had turned in my seat and my head was resting on Ricky's shoulder as I slowly opened my eyes when the bus came to a stop. He leaned over and told me it was time to get off the bus and take a walk.

"The legs need to be stretched and moved around or you can develop blood clots."

"Sounds like you've done this before." I said in my sleepy voice.

"Yeah, a few times. I enjoy this trip a lot. I meet interesting people and I enjoy the scenery, present company included." he answered with a grin.

As I stood up my lower back ached. I reached around to rub it. Ricky saw what I was doing and brushed my hand out of the way and proceeded to rub just above the waistband of my jeans. God that felt so good. I could have let him do that forever. But

I wanted to go into the terminal restroom and freshen up and change into my sweats for the nights ride. I could sleep better being more comfortable. So, I told him thank you for the back rub and I would see him when we got back on the bus.

Little did I know that Ricky had followed me and watched to make sure I got into the restroom with no problems. I did a quick sponge bath with baby wipes and shampooed my hair and dried it under the hand blow dryer. My hair came almost to the middle of my back and wasn't quite dry, so I pulled it up in a ponytail and tied it off with a band. I put on just a dab of makeup and changed into my purple nylon/rayon, fleece lined sweat suit. Putting back on my socks and sneakers I went back out into the terminal heading toward the restaurant. I was famished, having not eaten since Savannah earlier that afternoon. As soon as I turned the corner, out of the ladies' room, there was Ricky.

"Hi. Wow! I didn't think you could look any better, but you look fantastic." he said with a huge grin on his face. "May I escort you to wherever it is you are going next?"

"What are you doing...following me?" I asked him. I tried to look perturbed, but I couldn't. I really was kinda glad that he was there watching over me.

Being a single woman traveling alone and all....

"No, I just happened to come out of the men's room and saw you coming out of the ladies' room. So how about it? Can we go somewhere together and get something to eat? Are you hungry?"

The man could read my mind. "Sure. Where do you want to go? I'm starving."

"Well, we can grab a bite here in the terminal or we can go across the street and grab something to go and take it back and eat it on the bus. What would be your pleasure, ma'am?" Ricky still had a grin on his face.

"Well, let me see. The food in the terminals usually isn't very good. So, let's go across the street to the diner and get something to go," I answered with a smile.

"Damn baby, you sure are gorgeous when you smile," he said and leaned over and kissed me on the forehead. I was so surprised by the gesture that I stumbled as we moved toward the door. He took a hold of my arm and led me out and across the street.

We entered the diner and walked up to the counter. Looking at the menus, waiting for the waitress, I wondered what I should get that would be easy to eat on the bus.

As the waitress came over, she looked at us and said, "Well, what will it be, and you better hurry if you want to catch your bus." How did she know we were from the bus? I looked around the room and to my left sat the bus driver, finishing up his dinner and drinking his coffee.

"I'd like a cheeseburger all the way with French fries and a mountain dew in the bottle, to go, please." Ricky ordered the same.

As we waited for our food we dabbled in small talk. I discovered that he was on his way to Madeira, only a short way from Fresno. He was a lawyer in a small law firm with two other lawyers. They were primarily defense attorneys of criminal law. He was single, divorced recently with no children.

I told him I was also divorced recently, two months ago, and was on my way to my aunt's house in Fresno to restart my life. I told him that at the age of twenty-eight, I thought my life was pretty well set. But my husband had found a new "love of his life" and wanted out. So, I gave him his walking papers. I also told Ricky that I am a court stenographer, so we had a little something in common. We both know our way around a courtroom. The waitress brought us our food and Ricky insisted on paying for it, then we went back to the bus. We ate as the bus rumbled down the road.

After finishing eating, we both settled down with books and started reading. He with whatever it was he was reading and me with a good erotic romance. I noticed that every once in a while, he would slide a sideways look over at me. I would smile to myself as I kept on reading. I was into a really good part and was starting to get really warm when he reached over and took my hand in his. He kept on reading, content with holding hands. Almost two hours rolled by as we read and just held hands. It was very relaxing and with no pretensions.

Once in a while I would set my book in my lap, take a drink of soda, set the bottle between my legs and pick the book up and start reading again. The last time I did that he asked me,

"Is the book that good that you need to cool yourself off?"

"Um," (and I swallowed really hard), "it was just an easy place to put it, that's all."

"Aha," was all he said, and he went back to his book.

I couldn't stand it anymore. Between the book and this hot, gorgeous man sitting beside me I was getting so horny, so I put the book away, stood up and pulled my blanket and pillow from the overhead compartment and settled in to go to sleep. Putting the seat back, I stretched my legs out and tried my best to get comfortable in such cramped quarters.

The lady next to me was already fast asleep. She must have been in her sixties, graying hair and small in stature. Her feet barely touched the floor. I took the blanket and covered my shoulders, put my hands under the blanket to hold it in place, turned my head toward the lady and closed my eyes.

I was almost asleep when I felt Ricky's hand slip under the blanket and search for mine. He had turned in his seat and was leaning near me. As he grasped my hand, he leaned his head to my ear and kissed it. I moved my head slightly and he moved with it. He kissed it again. Then his tongue reached out and licked my neck. I turned my head slightly toward him, but he pushed it back with his head. Again, he licked my neck.

"Boy, this guy has some nerve." I thought. "We just met today, and he is already trying to neck with me."

About the time I was thinking this, Ricky let go of my hand and reached up and cupped my chin. Turning my head towards him he planted his lips on mine. At first, I was so stunned that I couldn't react. His lips were soft. So tender that I wanted them to stay there. So, I kissed him back. His tongue reached out to caress my lower lip, teasing, pressing it a little then he bit it lightly. I moaned. Oh, God. What was he doing to me? I started to put up my hand to protest. Quickly he held my head and pressed his lips to mine harder and pushed with his tongue until I opened mouth and let him in. Oh My God he tasted so good. He was ravishing my mouth. Touching my teeth, my gums, the inside of my cheeks. He was hungry for my mouth. His hand slipped down my head to my neck and on down to my shoulder and under the covers. I brought my hand up to his face and it felt soft, only a little rough where his beard was starting to have a day's growth. I held his mouth to mine and kissed him back.... oh, he felt so good and wonderful. I put my tongue into his mouth and explored it as he had in mine.

I felt his hand go lower down to my left breast. He was massaging it through my sweatshirt.... God it felt great. It had been over a year since any man had touched me. My nipples were getting hard and I could feel the twinge in my vagina. Ricky reached down under my shirt and lifted it up so he could get to my breasts better. I had left my bra off so I could relax and be more comfortable for sleeping. Now he had full access.

He massaged my breast and then played with my nipple as he continued to kiss me fervently, feverishly. I was starting to squirm in my seat. He released our kiss and whispered in my ear to be quiet.

"Hush baby. Just enjoy this. Don't wake up our little lady over there."

I turned my body toward him. He reached around me, held me and kissed me again, hard and passionately. I reached up and put my fingers in his hair. It was soft and felt like silk in my hand. I played in it, pulled it to pull him closer to me.

I wanted him now. I wanted him to do to me whatever he wanted to. I moaned into his mouth. He returned the moan with a groan from deep in his throat. His feet tangled with mine and he was going up and down my calf with his bare foot. He must have kicked off his shoes sometime, I thought to myself. So, I kicked mine off too. We let our feet play with each other's legs while he played with first one breast and then the other.

God, I was getting so hot!!! He was turning me on so much!!!

His hand then started downward toward my stomach, down my abdomen and to my curly bush. He went under the waistband of my sweatpants. With his long slender hand and his fingers, he played in my cunt hair and moved on down to my pussy.

OH MY GOD!!!! As his fingers hit my clitoris I jumped and a slow, low moan emitted from my lips.

"Hush baby, it's ok...just take it easy. Enjoy the ride." Ricky whispered into my ear again.

That was easier said than done. He was making me burn down there. I wanted more....

"Please Ricky, take me...make me cum. Please baby..." I begged him.

"I will baby, I will. Just take it easy ...relax and let me take care of you, hot stuff. My God, you are so hot...your pussy is on fire darling."

Ricky was driving me crazy with desire. He let his fingers go down deeper into my slit clear back to my pucker hole. I was so wet that his fingers just slid down, so easily, and back up again. He was teasing the shit out of me. Then I felt two fingers go inside me. My hips automatically went up in the air. He put his other arm around my shoulders and pulled me into him and held me as he started pumping his fingers in and out of my pussy. I was so wet he was sliding in and out and moving his fingers around inside of me.

He pushed his fingers up on my gspot and flicked his fingers faster and faster.

He pinched my clit...

"Oh..." Ricky plunged a kiss on my lips to quiet my cry as I came with an explosion.... a burst of lightening going off in the sky. Each stroke he made seemed to keep the climax going a little bit longer. I soaked his fingers and my cum ran down his hand. I was holding on to him for dear life.

Ricky didn't take his fingers out of me but kept playing. He wiggled them around, in and out and up against my gspot again. He twirled around my clit and pinched it again. As I slid down on the seat, he flicked his little finger along my pucker hole, and I exploded again. Intense, deep, cumming with so much force he had all he could do to smother my screams with his mouth.

I was cumming so hard I reached out to grab something and grabbed his cock. He was so hard. And so big. As I slowly receded from the best climax I had had in a very long time, I knew this awesome man deserved to be taken care of as well.

As I rubbed my hand back and forth his cock swelled and I knew I wanted to have him. Quickly I unbuttoned his jeans and slid down the zipper. I moved the blanket around so that some of it was covering his lap as well as mine. I then took out the most beautiful cock I had ever seen. God, it was huge, and the head was thick and moist from his precum. Oh, I love the taste of precum and couldn't wait to get my lips on his engorged meat.

I lowered my head and put out my tongue and licked the tip of his cock. Ricky let out a low groan. He buried his head in my hair and I continued to lick his stick like a mad woman. He tasted so good. I opened my mouth and put the head into it, and he moaned. His hand went into my hair as he held my head to his dick. I worked my way down his lovely shaft until I had most of it gone. I started to gag. He was too big for my mouth and throat. But again, I tried to take all of him. After several attempts, I finally was able to take him to the hilt. My nose was buried all the way into his pubic hair. He didn't hold me there though and I bobbed up and down his rod until I could feel his cum rising up from his balls. Up the shaft it came and into my mouth. I swallowed rope after rope of cum as he squirted into my throat. I sucked him until I knew that I had drained him of all his juices. Then I raised my head and looked at him.

He had that huge grin on his face, but this time I was glad to see it there. He grabbed hold of my face and kissed me deeply, tasting himself as he did. A deep groan came from down deep in his chest and came into my mouth. He bit at my lips...he sucked them and kissed me some more.

Ricky's fingers had never left my cunt and he was once again playing inside of me. I was still soaking wet from my previous orgasm, so he was able to move about easily. In and out he moved his fingers. Then his thumb found my clit and he started rubbing it. Gently at first and then harder and harder while never missing a beat as he pumped me with his fingers. I knew I was going to cum again. I pushed my pants down to just below my hips, while still covered by the blanket.

Ricky turned more towards me and held me tight while he pumped my pussy like a man possessed. I bit into his shoulder as I came, and came, and came. The flow of my juices went all over his hand and wrist. Still, he didn't stop. I was so turned on I thought I was in heaven. I reached over and touched his cock and he was hard as a rock again.

"Come over here and sit on my lap. Carefully, so we don't wake up the little lady, said Ricky.

I was too far gone to argue with him...besides. I wanted his cock in my pussy so bad. So, he held up the blanket for me to move over onto his lap. He had pulled his jeans down and I pulled my sweats down to my ankles.

Although it was rather awkward, we managed to get it where I was straddling him, and I sat down with his cock aimed for my opening. He held my lips open with one hand and guided his cock with the other into my cunt.

"Oh, God, you are so big." I whispered. He was stretching me and stretching me. Even with being so wet and loosened up, he was making me so full.

We worked back and forth, in and out until he was all the way in me. God, I was stuffed. I didn't think I could take someone that big...ever. Well, tonight I found out different.

Ricky was moving ever so slowly, letting me get use to his size. He felt wonderful. We were trying to be as quiet as possible, but it was so difficult when it felt this good.

Soon we had worked out a rhythm that felt good to us and we were enjoying each other. Just then the old lady stirred and started mumbling. We held very still. Waiting...she finally settled back down and started snoring again.

Slowly Ricky started moving in and out as I moved up and down. This was ecstasy as its best. I never wanted it to end. But I was on the verge of a huge climax. Damn, he was good at doing that to me. I never got this much enjoyment in the whole eight years I was married, let alone get it now with a total stranger I've known just a few hours.

Ricky pulled me back into his chest and wrapped his arms around me. Then he started pumping his cock into me rapidly and I went off. Burst after burst of fulfillment went through me and I was propelled into another realm of reality.

I felt as his cock got stiffer and bigger and as he started squirting his cum deep up into my vagina, right into my cervix. Deeply he pumped his juices of maleness into me, over and over.

So much that it was leaking out of me. Our combined juices were creaming us. I pushed my fist into my mouth to stifle my scream of joy.

God, this man was one hell of a great lover. I kept my head on his shoulder and rested against his chest. Cuddled in his arms, he kissed me gently on my head and I smiled. I really smiled for the first time in a long time. My whole being was relaxed and happy. Within a few seconds I was sound asleep, still in Ricky's lap, his meat still inside of me.

Light was just starting to come in through the window of the bus when I slowly opened my eyes. I was still on Ricky's lap and to my amazement his cock was still inside of me and was very hard. I moved slightly to see if he was awake. Oh yes, he certainly was. He gave me a jab with his cock, straight up. I jumped a little and he chuckled.

"Good morning, hot stuff. I hope you slept well. I know I sure did." Ricky said with a grin.

I turned my head to look up at him and I saw a set of eyes looking straight at us. I sat straight up...forgetting to pull the blanket up with me.

"Oops, sorry." I said as I pulled it around us.

"Oh, no need to be sorry dear. I heard everything last night. I'm sure glad you enjoyed yourselves and it was me sitting here and not some snooty old biddy who would have raised a ruckus with you. But I would suggest you put yourselves back together before the other passengers start rousing from their stupor. Might be a little embarrassing, if you know what I mean." The little old lady hid a giggle, excused herself and headed for the restroom.

NO NAME

"**O**h, baby, you feel so good! I love having my cock buried so deep in your pussy," the stranger said as he pumped his dick in and then slowly out of me.

I laid there not knowing why my body was reacting to his cock stroking me. I was getting so wet and I could feel a climax nearing the more he pushed. He went so deep, clear to my womb. His body was slippery from the sweat he was causing to build up between us. He nibbled on my neck and ear, kissed my neck. Then he reached between us and took hold of my clitoris and pinched it between his fingers.

"Ohhhh Gooodddd...nnnooooo, please," I cried.

He was bringing me to the most intense climax I could remember ever having. I tried to move away from him, but his weight was too much. I couldn't move my arms, they were tied and held above my head....my legs were held out to the sides and I couldn't move them either. What the hell was going on? And who was this man lying on top of me?

Suddenly I felt him grow bigger inside of me and he started pulsing. I felt a warm liquid deep in my cunt. He moaned as he spurted over and over again, seeming never to end.

Finally, he rolled over to his side with one leg and arm still across me. He cuddled me and held me as if I was his only love.

I lay there in total confusion. Who was he, why was he in my house and why was he having sex with me? He raped me...yet he was so gentle and caring. He made sure that I reached my climax before he did. It's so dark in here I can't see him. He had made sure all the lights were off and the shades were all pulled. Not a hint of light was shining in my bedroom.

When I woke up there was light shining through the shaded bedroom window. My arms and legs were still tied and in the same position as they were before I went to sleep. I was really wet between my legs in my private area and the stranger was asleep beside me. And I really had to go use the bathroom.

The stranger looked over at me, smiled, pulled his hand through his thick black hair and sat up putting his legs over the side of the bed.

"Good morning sweet thing," he said with a grin on his face.

He had the most beautiful smile and the whitest set of teeth I had ever seen. As he stood up his lean body was taut with muscles that bulged from his wide chest and thick thighs. He had washboard abs and arms that would rival any body builder. As he turned to walk toward the bathroom he stopped and looked at me.

"Do you have to use the bathroom darlin'? I bet you do after all that lovin' last night."

He came back to the bed and started untying the ropes on my arms one at a time. As they came down, I rubbed them trying to get the circulation going again. He then went to the bottom of the bed and undid the ties on my ankles. Slowly I sat up in bed and rubbed my legs to the ankles. I felt so stiff and sore from being in that position for so long. I looked around me to see if there was any way I could get away from him, but he knew what I was thinking.

"Don't try to go anywhere but to the bathroom over there babe."

The stranger had a firm look in his deep brown eyes that told me not to take any risks or I would truly be sorry. So, I walked carefully to the bathroom and closed the door behind me. Letting out a deep breath, I just wanted to sit there and cry.

"Just do your little potty thing sweetie and be quick about it." he said through the door.

As soon as I was finished, I opened the door to him standing there waiting for me. I looked up into his eyes and he stared back into mine. Then a slight grin formed across his face. He turned me around and led me back into the bathroom.

"Why are you bringing me back in here?" I asked not sure what he was up to.

"Well, I can't very well leave you out there by yourself, now can I? So, you'll have to sit in here with me while I relieve myself and then we are going to take a shower together. We're both pretty messy after such good lovin' last night. And oh baby, it was great."

"Who are you and why are you doing this to me?" I asked him as I sat on the edge of the bathtub while he urinated.

As he finished, he turned to me, pulled me up by my shoulders and looked at me softly and answered.

"Because you are the most beautiful, sensual woman I have ever seen. I have watched you for a very long time and couldn't wait any longer to make you totally mine. Your body is so soft and supple. Your breasts are so pert, and your nipples peak so well at my touch. I like to suck on them and bite on them like this." He bent down and put his lips to her right breast and took her nipple into his mouth and suckled it gently, lovingly, worshiping her.

My hands reached into his hair and held his head as he loved on my breast...then he moved to the other one and continued the same treatment. I felt myself getting wet as his hands roamed over my back and down my hips. God, he felt so good. How can I let this man whom, I don't even know do these things to my body?

We both let out low moans at the same time. He then raised his head and kissed me, gently at first then pushing his tongue into my mouth and devouring me. I returned his kiss with as much as he gave. We warred each other with our tongues, teasing and tasting one another.

The sensations I was feeling were overwhelming and I wanted more. My body was craving him.... needing him. God, I'm losing it.... how can I want someone who is taking me against my will, by force...or is he?

Suddenly he stopped, pulled up and just stood there. He looked confused, like he didn't know what he wanted to do next. Then he slowly looked at me and pointed to the shower.... my eyes followed, and I knew what he wanted.

So, I went to the walk-in shower and opened the glass door. I stepped inside and turned and looked back at him. He was right behind me. As he stepped in, he grabbed me around my waist and turned me around so that my back was to his chest. He turned the water on and adjusted the temperature to make it nice and warm. He held me close as the water cascaded down from my breasts, down my stomach and over my patch of pubic hair.

The stranger reached up and grasped both breasts in his hands and started massaging them and tweaking my nipples. I could feel his hardness against my ass cheeks and my lower back.

His hands slowly traveled down over my stomach and splayed over my mons, barely reaching into my vaginal area. He played there for a short time while I kept feeling his manhood growing and pulsing behind me. I knew I was getting really wet. He then stopped and turned me around and put my head under the water and wet my hair. Taking the shampoo, he put some into his hand and worked it into my hair, massaging my scalp. Oh Lord, it felt so good. I relaxed at his ministrations. He rinsed out the soap and put in the cream rinse.

With some of the cream rinse still on his hands he reached down and started working his fingers back and forth over my pussy lips, inserting first one and then two fingers into me. My legs started to wobble with the intensity of how hot he was getting me. He grabbed hold of me around my waist with one arm and I leaned into him to keep my balance. I was coming unglued. It seemed like every part of my body was on fire.

How could this be happening to me. I don't even know this man, yet he has managed to turn me to putty in his hands. I couldn't resist any longer.

As I neared my climax I reached for his cock, which was so hard, and stroked it with my fist tight around it. He moaned loudly as I screamed with my release.

My knees buckled, and he grabbed me tighter, holding me up and closer to his body.

"Ohhhh mmmyyyyy Goooddddd.......please stop.... I can't take any more." I reached for his hand, trying to slow down the motion of his fingers in my cunt but he kept up the pace, not relenting.

His thumb on my clit kept circling and circling. I felt like I was going to faint and then everything started to go hazy......

When I came to, he had carried me and laid me on the bed. He was looking down at my face while he brushed my hair and rubbed my neck.

"What happened and how did I get here on the bed?" I asked as I tried to get my vision back.

"You, my dear, had one gigantic orgasm. I would venture to say the best one you have ever had in your entire life and you passed out." explained the stranger.

I started to cry. The tears flowed down my face as he looked at me frowning.

"Why are you crying my sweet pet? You just had one fantastic orgasm and your crying. I don't get it." He had a forlorn look on his face. He really didn't understand.

"Look," I started explaining. "I haven't had sex in almost two years. Then I wake up to you being on top of me giving me the best sex I've ever had. I don't know who you are and why you are here. Yet, we have clicked so well, and you have made my body do things that my late husband never could. He didn't take the time to try." By then I was crying uncontrollably.

The stranger reached out and took me in his arms and held me close to his body. I tried to push away but he just held me that much tighter. I cried until I couldn't cry any longer. He then gently laid me down, went to the bathroom and came back with a warm wet washcloth and washed off my face.

"Do you feel better now?" he asked. "You seem to have had a lot of feelings built up inside that needed to come out."

"I'm sorry. You didn't deserve that. It's not your problem." I said back to him with a sigh.

"It seems to me that it became my problem when I came into this room. You are one hell of a woman. You are sensitive, responsive beyond belief, one of the most desirable women I have ever known."

"And do you meet all your women by appearing in their bedrooms and raping them?" I asked not daring to look at him.

"No, I do not. Someday, I will tell you why I am here, but not now. Because, right now, I want only to make you forget everything you have ever known about pain, sorrow, grief, sadness, and men who didn't know how to make you feel like a completed woman."

I slowly raised my eyes to look into his. He had the most honest looking eyes I had ever seen.

He took my hand and put it on his chest as he lowered his lips to mine. Tenderly our lips met. Neither of us moved. As he held my head his tongue licked at my lower lip, going back and forth until I opened my mouth and let his tongue in to explore every inch, along my teeth, over my gums, deeper in as if he was trying to push all the way down my throat. His kiss went from gentle to firm, hard to devouring. He wanted every inch of my mouth. He explored me, memorizing my mouth.

Finally, he broke away and looked into my eyes. We didn't have to say anything. No words were needed. He reached up and touched my breast as his head bent to kiss along my neck. My body was igniting with intense desire. He bit my ear and then licked it. Oh, God he was driving me wild. He leaned back again and looked at me intently.

Taking both breasts in his hands he massaged them and played with the nipples, pulling on them making them hard and pointing straight out. Each time he pulled I could feel tingles going straight into my cunt. Oh, I was getting so wet.

"Aaahhhhh, please," I moaned as he manipulated and played with my breasts. He lowered his head and took my right breast in his mouth.

"OOOOHHHH......that feels soooo good...." I cried.

He continued from one breast to the other for what seemed like forever. He moved and kissed down over my belly all the way down over my pubic hair to my pussy. He pulled my lips apart and licked between them from my puckered little hole to my clit in one slow move.

"Oh Lord Jesus....you are killing me........aaahhhhh." I couldn't contain the feelings he was causing in my body.

My hips raised to meet him as if they had a mind all their own. My body couldn't stay still. I reached and took hold of his head with both hands, pulling on his hair. Pushing his face into my cunt as I couldn't get enough. He licked me over and over again staying away from my clit.

His tongue stiffened, and he inserted it into my vagina. Each time he went in he went a little deeper...sucking me, drinking me, loving me.... when his thumb hit my clit, I exploded. My juices ran all over his tongue and face. He lapped at my pussy fast and furiously getting every drop of my succulent body fluid that he could get.

He eased up off my clit but kept his tongue in my hole as he started fingering my little cherry butt hole. Wow...this was a totally new feeling. It felt so good...

My hips gyrated, pushed up to meet his face and buried him in deeper. Then as his thumb hit my clit his little finger went inside my little hole.

"Holy   Mother   Mary.......... GGGOOOOOOOOOODDDDDDDDDDDD!!!!" I screamed!!!!!

Blast after blast hit me and I just kept cumming and cumming.......I soaked him, me and the sheet. It took forever for me to come down from the high he had put me on. When he finally lifted his head and looked up at me, he had a big grin on his face.

"Did you like that baby? Are you ready for round two?"

"Please, let me rest. That was overwhelmingly fantastic." I said as I smiled back down at him.

"Oh, no baby, that was only the beginning. "

I tried to wiggle away from him, but he grabbed a hold of my thighs and pulled me tighter to him.

"No way madame, you still have a lot to learn and we are far from through." He then lowered his head and started licking on my pussy lips again. He went for my pucker hole and swirled his tongue around and around it. I squirmed and moved my hips around. God he was good. He knew just where to go to get my body to respond to him. He then inserted two fingers into my other hole and moved them in and out at a slow pace. My hips started moving with him, up and down to his in and out. The pace went steady for a while and then he started curling his fingers upward and pressing on something inside me. His fingers started moving faster and faster. It started to feel like I had to pee. All of the sudden I felt a warm liquid running out of me and down his hand and my leg. My hips were out of control.... I couldn't stop, I didn't want him to stop...I pulled his hair, I yelled like I wanted everyone to hear me.

"Don't   stop....   don't   stop......yesses..........
uuuuuuuuuuuuuuhhhhhhh!!!"

The stranger grabbed my thighs and held on to me, but never once let off. He kept me going and going and going. His pinky was working its way in and out of my rectum as his middle and index fingers were pumping in and out of my cunt.

And his tongue was going wild over my clit. He was driving me into another realm of reality. My lips were so swollen from his ministrations and the blood flowing into them. I was in utopia and never wanted to come back.

When he finally moved, I didn't realize it until he was sitting on my chest with his cock in his hand. Slowly, he was stroking it back and forth. As I looked up at him, I knew what he wanted. I had never been one to like sucking on a man's penis. Now, here it was, right in my face and he wanted me to suck on him. After what he just did for me, I did owe him that much, didn't I?

As he leaned closer, I stuck out my tongue and licked the tip. He already had pre-cum dripping from it, so I licked at it several times. It didn't taste so bad. I got a little braver and licked all around the engorged head. He jerked a little. I took notice that I had caused that. So, I did it again. And again, it jumped.

Damn, I thought, I do have some control of what happens with his cock, don't I? As I stuck my tongue out again, he reached out and touched my chin. So, I opened my mouth and he pushed forward until the tip of his penis was starting to enter my mouth. I closed my lips around his tip and sucked a little. He let out a low moan. We kept our eyes on each other as I opened my mouth again and took a little bit more of him. His groan was a little bit louder this time.

God, I never knew I could have this effect on a man. My husband was not this gentle and all he wanted was to jam it in my mouth and get off quick. This stranger wanted to savor the feeling. He was definitely enjoying himself.

"Well then, let's let him really enjoy it," I thought.

So, I kept opening my mouth and taking a little more of him each time. Finally, I had him to right at the beginning of my throat. I gagged a little and he backed off some. He kept slowly inching deeper until I was able to take all of his 8 inches. Then he pumped his hips back and forth while holding my head still. I had a couple of gag moments and he would stop until I had it back under control and then he would start out slowly again and build up the pace.

"Ah baby, your mouth feels like heaven. You are a great cock sucker darlin," he said as he kept a steady pace. "But I'm gonna cum in your mouth if we keep this up and I don't want to do that. I'm not finished with you yet."

So, he pulled out of my mouth, backed down my body and leaned over and kissed me hard. He was devouring me. As he was, he positioned himself between my legs and put his cock up to my pussy lips and pushed in all the way to the hilt. We both let out a deep moan at the same time. God, he felt so good filling me all the way up my cunt. He was so big....so hard.... I wanted him more than I had ever wanted any man.

"Baby fuck me.......please......fuck me hard. Make me cum!!!!!!!!I want you so much. You feel soooo goood...." I couldn't get enough of him.

The stranger reached down and pulled up my legs and held them by my calves bending me almost in half and he pounded me. He gave me all that he had. Our eyes were focused only on each other.

We knew nothing but what we were at that moment. I felt his cock get huge inside me and then he came....and I came...... all over him.... him deep inside of me.... pulse after pulse.... hot semen into my womb.... we were one .... together.

We slept for hours wrapped in each other's arms. The stranger woke before me and was already showered and dressed.

I asked him why he was dressed, and he said it was time for him to leave.

"Why? Can't you stay a while longer? I've gotten kinda use to you being here."

"No, my dearest. My time here is over. I've done what I was sent here to do. You will be fine now."

"What are you talking about? Who sent you?" none of this was making any sense.

"I'm an Angel and God knew how much difficulty you've been having adjusting since the death of your husband. I was sent here to let you know that you are a great and wonderful woman who can be happy again. All you need is to believe in yourself. I think you can now do that. So, it is now time for me to go back to my Heavenly home. But I will miss you. You are one hot, sexy lady."

With that the Stranger was gone. I blinked my eyes and thought to myself,,,,,,,,,

"I didn't even know his name!!!!!!!!!!!"

DOCTOR KEVIN

Today was Shannon's birthday, her 35th birthday to be exact. Long ago I had run out of ideas of what to get her and each year was getting harder and harder. This was definitely a milestone birthday and what in blue blazes was I going to get her.

"Honey don't forget that I'm going to the doctor for my yearly exam today," Shannon called to me from the master bathroom. "You'll have to pick up Cassidy (our 8-year-old daughter) from the sitters after you get off work, okay?"

"Sure doll, at Marissa's, right?" I asked her to make sure I had the right sitter.

"Yes, Kevin. She's been our only sitter for the last six months," Shannon answered me as she was walking into our master bedroom looking like a million bucks.

I was still laying on our king size bed in just my boxer shorts and my male body part immediately came to attention.

"Wow baby, you look fantastic. You always go to the doctor dressed like that?" I asked her as my cock got even harder.

"What?" she asked with a sheepish grin on her beautiful face.

Shannon had on a slim, tight fitting black stretch skirt and a vee neck pull over red and white long-sleeved sweater that showed her well-endowed chest off perfectly.

"I suppose you have on a thong too." I asked her.

"Kevin, it's not like the doctor will care. He does these exams every day of the week, all day long. It's just another one to him. Don't get so bent out of shape about it. We go through this every year baby. Nothing to worry about. Besides, he won't see the thong because I will be completely nude. Well, except for that little paper gown I have to put on."

Oh, that made me feel a whole lot better. Shannon tried to coax me down a little but there was another man going to look at my wife's pussy.

Oh My God...I hate this. Wonder what it does to her though? What does it do to her?? How does she feel when he's looking around inside her and touching her there? Oh God...

Kevin decided that he needed some answers as to what exactly happened inside that room during an examination and he knew just who to ask. Janis Clayton, a nurse at another doctor's office, lived across the hall from them.

Later that morning he spotted her in the parking lot getting ready to leave for work. Kevin flew down the stairs and just made it to her car in time to stop her.

"Kevin, what is it? Are you okay?" asked Janis.

"Yeah, I'm fine but I have a huge question to ask you and please don't slap me or think I'm getting too personal. Okay?" God, this was going to be strange.

"Okay, Kevin. Whatever it is it can't be that bad. What's going on? Are Shannon and Cassidy okay?" she asked.

"Yeah, they're fine. Okay, here goes. Shannon has her yearly female exam today and I ...well...I was wondering what all goes on and how it feels to her. I mean is it painful or does she get embarrassed or what? And how can the doctor look at all those pussies...I mean cunts...I mean.... you know without getting a hard-on."

Man, I felt like my face was beet red. I hope I didn't embarrass her and/or myself too much. But damn it, I wanted to know.

Janis sat in her beige-colored Camry car seat and stared at me for what seemed like an eternity but was really only a second or two and then a smile spread across her face.

"Well, first of all, I guess the doctor is just immune to pussy. Except for his wife I suppose. Secondly, no, a woman doesn't usually enjoy it very much. I mean first, the doctor mauls her breasts looking for lumps and then has her spread her legs wide open and shoves a speculum up her twat and spreads her insides open and gawks up there. Then he takes it out...shoves his finger up there and then up her ass, tells her she is fine and leaves the room. Now, does that sound like a lot of fun to you? Have a great day Kevin and quit worrying so much." she finished with a huff.

Kevin thought a minute and as she started to pull out, he hit the car to stop her again.

"Janis, could you do me a huge favor?"

Later that night after Kevin, Shannon and Cassidy had gone out for a fantastic dinner and a surprise birthday cake at Shannon's mothers, Cassidy wanted to spend the night with her Nana.

"Great idea. Of course, you can," answered Kevin before anyone had a chance to even think about it.

Once they were home Kevin escorted Shannon up to their huge master bathroom and fixed her a relaxing hot bath. While she was in there, he prepared the bedroom for her birthday surprise. The items, which he had asked Janis to get for him were neatly lined up on the nightstand and covered with a small lavender colored hand towel.

He quickly changed into the green scrubs which Janis had also brought for him. Just as he had finished, he heard Shannon climbing out of the bathtub and let the water drain out. As she was drying off, she asked Kevin to bring her the turquoise nightgown hanging on the hook in her walk-in closet.

"Oh, you won't be needing it tonight dear. I hung a robe on the hook on the back of the bathroom door. If you would, kindly put it on and come into the bedroom please." Kevin told her with a smile on his face from ear to ear.

The white silky robe Shannon found behind the door was short sleeved and as she put it on, she noticed that it barely covered her ass cheeks and left not much hidden in the front either. As she left the bathroom to enter their bedroom, she saw Kevin waiting for her wearing a set of green scrubs.

"Kevin, why are you wearing those scrubs? She asked.

"Well, my name is Doctor Kevin madame. Tonight, you are going to be given your yearly exam. I want you to be as comfortable as possible. Relax and find as much enjoyment as I can give you. If you are ready, please lay on the exam bed on the towels provided."

Shannon looked at her husband as if he had lost his last marble in his so-called brain. "What on earth are you doing?"

"Please madame, just recline on the bed so we can start with your exam."

Kevin assisted Shannon down into a reclined position upon the lavender towels he had laid out on the bed, putting a pillow under her head and her arms down to her sides. Picking up a clipboard with a piece of paper attached, he started.

"Well, Mrs. Abbott, it says here that today is your 35th birthday. Congratulations. How have you been feeling? Any problems with sexual intercourse, any breast pain or lumps, etc.? Okay, we will start with the breast exam. I'm going to open the left side of your robe and feel around your left breast for anything abnormal."

Kevin moved the robe aside and started massaging her left breast. Shannon was dumbfounded. Kevin started out doing it like he was actually feeling for lumps or anything out of the ordinary. But then he started going into a deeper massage and then began to rub her nipple and twirl it in between his fingers. Her nipple immediately hardened in reaction to his touch.

"Very good reaction with your breast and nipple Mrs. Abbott. Now I am going to move your right side of the robe open and do the same thing to your right breast."

And thus, he did. Shannon was almost to the point of moaning. In fact, she did stifle a couple of almost silent ones and felt tingling all the way down to her mound.

"Oh, Kevin...what are you doing? This isn't what really happens." Shannon was starting to protest but Kevin quickly quieted her back down and told her to relax.

"Both breasts seem to be quite normal. Both are very reactive to stimuli and that is very good indeed."

He could see Shannon squirming around the bed a little bit as she was getting turned on by this little exam he was doing to her. He turned and smiled to himself as he made little notations on the paper attached to the clipboard. Yup...this is going to be fun he thought to himself.

"Mrs. Abbott, it is now time for me to do the pelvic exam on you. I know this is not the most welcome part, but it is a necessity, so please place your feet on the mattress with your knees bent up. Spread your legs open so I can see and examine your pelvic area."

Kevin moved to the bottom of the bed. As Shannon placed her feet on the mattress and bent her knees, Kevin put on a pair of latex gloves and got the k-y jelly ready.

"Okay, madame, I'm going to feel around your vaginal lips and your clitoris if you are ready?"

Shannon almost wanted to laugh at the seriousness of how Kevin was trying to carry out this exam. But, God, it was feeling so damn good. How could she stop him... why would she stop him?

"Yes, doctor. I'm ready." She figured she would play along.

That said, Kevin applied a small amount of the lubricant on his gloved fingers, he didn't need much as she was already getting pretty wet on her own and started rubbing on either side of her clitoris. The lips were so warm, and she moved her hips in response to his timulation. Purposely Kevin stayed away from her clitoris and massaged her from the top to her little pucker hole. Her hips rotated and moved up into his hand as he stimulated her. He then inserted his index finger into her and her hips rose up to meet him, wanting him even deeper into her.

"OMG", Shannon thought....it never felt like this at her doctor's office.

Slowly he pulled out his finger. "Mrs. Abbott, I must now insert the speculum so that I can look inside of your vagina to make sure you are healthy in there. Are you ready?"

"Kevin, you aren't really going to do that, are you?"

Before she could think of anything else, Kevin had the instrument already just inside her pussy and was starting to push it in. Shannon's eyes went huge and she tried to lift up to see what he was doing to her.

"Please Mrs. Abbott, remain laying down. I do not want to hurt you with this speculum inside of you. It will be over in just a moment or two."

Kevin continued opening the speculum wider inside his wife's vagina and then got down lower on the floor, so he could look inside.

"Wow...so this is what it looks like inside her," he thought to himself.

He could see her cervix, uterus, the walls of her insides... right where his cock felt so warm and at home. He saw where his seed entered going through the cervix to enter her uterus where an egg could be made into a baby...like his little Cassidy.

Kevin stared at her in awe. "My beautiful, gorgeous wife. She's breathtaking from the inside out." His thoughts went straight to his groin and his cock was so hard he thought it would break.

"You're doing just fine Mrs. Abbott. I'm going to remove the speculum now. I still have to do an internal examination with my fingers inserted into your vagina. This shouldn't be too uncomfortable."

Slowly Kevin inserted his index and middle fingers into her and Shannon felt herself stretching to accommodate him. As he was going in deeper, pushing on the little walnut at the top of her vaginal wall he reached up with his thumb and started massaging her lips on either side of her clitoris. Shannon couldn't hold her hips still and started rotating them trying to make him have contact with her clit.

"Oh God, please. I want to cum." she heard herself crying out to Kevin.

"Now, now madame, just relax. You are showing all the natural reactions of stimuli. This shows me that you are indeed a normal, healthy woman."

Shannon shook from the red-hot fire of desire she was feeling.

Getting his pinky finger wet from the juices she was secreting he started rubbing her puckered hole. Shannon jumped at the contact and then it started to feel good. As he massaged it, he felt it relax a bit and inserted his finger into the hole. At the same time, he hit her clit with his thumb pushing Shannon into a climax so hard she had stars in her eyes. Kevin continued to fuck her ass as he rubbed her clit and plunged the two fingers into her pussy. Shannon's hips slammed into his hand over and over as she rode out her climax until it subsided and left her panting and breathless.

Kevin could stand it no more. He stood up, removed the latex gloves from his hands, bent over his wife and pushed his cock into her until he was deep into her cunt. He held still and relished in the feel of her as her vaginal muscles tightened around him. Then he slowly pulled back out almost leaving her warmth and pushed back in all the way again. Her moans were deeper than he had ever heard from her. He built up a rhythm of in and out until he was pounding her pussy with all he had to give. Shannon was matching him hip to hip, pubic bone to pubic bone until they both cried out together and came with a power they hadn't known or felt in a long time. Kevin ejaculated inside of her three, four, five times before he had totally emptied his balls. Shannon shook with a fervor that took several minutes to calm back down. Each had reached a pinnacle of completeness beyond their comprehension. Kevin eased off of her and rolled onto his back taking her with him and she cuddled and rested her head on his chest.

"Baby, that was the most awesome experience I have ever had in my life." stated Kevin when he had caught his breath again.

"If my real exam had been like that, believe me I would have been there more than once a year." Shannon knew he would react to that statement and here it came.

"I don't think you need to go there anymore. One Doctor looking inside you is enough, and I can do the job just fine."

They both laughed and made passionate love the rest of the night.

NEW KIND OF LOVE

"Want a woman to text with....any subject... it's your choice."

The ad stuck out at me like a sore thumb. This guy wants to talk to women about anything. Hum. So, I clicked on the ad and read it. Wow!!! This can't be real. A guy actually finds talking with women exciting. As I was having a lonely, quiet, boring evening I decided to answer his ad.

"Hi, this is Gigi. So, you want to do girl talk? Why? What is it you want to know about us? "

Curiosity was killing me about a guy who wanted to spend his time talking to women. What was he about? Well, let's see if he answers me. I hit the send button.

Within ten minutes I heard the ding that I had received an email. Sure enough it was from him.

"Hi, my name is Jake. Yes, I love talking to women. They are a most interesting species. I don't care what you look like or how old you are. Only that you truly are a female. No subject is taboo, and we can talk as often as you like. I do prefer to use text rather than email, if that is acceptable with you. Here is my number...I hope to hear from you soon. Tell me what is on your mind right now baby."

Oh My God!!!! This guy is for real, I think. He wants to hear from me by text. Okay, let's give this a try, I said to Nikki my Maltese dog who was laying at the foot of my bed.

After I entered his name to my contact list, I hit message and text:

"Hi Jake, it's Gigi. Now you have my number. Well, I'm sitting here on my bed with my little Maltese Nikki and writing to you. This is the first time I have ever answered an ad like this, so I'm not really sure where to start.

"Right now I'm bored out of my mind. I don't really like to watch tv, don't have a good book to read and no date."

"So, you're sitting or lying on your bed all alone?"

"Yeah, bummer, huh. What a way to spend a Friday night."

"You don't have a boyfriend or anyone special in your life?"

"No, we broke up about a month ago. Why are you home on a Friday night?"

"Actually, I'm at work. I watch monitors and it gets pretty boring, so I text."

"Do you have a girlfriend or significant other?"

"Nope...not anymore. Too many complications. Now I get to talk to you. Love it."

"Cool...so what do we talk about.... let's see, I'm sure you don't want to hear about my going shopping or what color I want to paint the kitchen."

"Well, do you like to cook...do you spend much time in the kitchen? It should be a color you feel comfortable in... warm... relaxing. Do you have a glass of wine while you cook? What do you wear while you are in there?"

"Why is all of that important?"

"Because, my dear, a kitchen can be just as romantic as the bedroom. Think about it. What and how you cook sets the mood for the rest of the evening. What you wear puts you in either a relaxed mood or in a hurry. If you wear short shorts and a halter top, drink a little wine and have on some really cool music your mind can conjure up some mighty fine dishes. You've also set the ambiance for your guest or mate to satisfy his pallet as well as his eyes. Loving is not done just in the bedroom."

"I suppose next you're going to tell me to cook with a negligee on."

"If that suits the situation, by all means yes.... wow what a turn on."

"Hum...never thought of it that way. Well, it's late and I have to work in the morning so am going to go. Nice talking to you, Jake."

"Yeah, you too Gigi. Hope we can talk again. You seem like a really nice person."

I thought about Jake all day. I couldn't get him off my mind. I had only talked with him for a few minutes, yet he intrigued me. What was it about him? Why did he want to talk to me of all people? And his ideas of the kitchen were kind of a turn on. Yep...I wanted to talk with Jake some more. I definitely wanted to know more about this guy and what made him tick.

Quickly I changed my clothes, grabbed my cell and made sure it was fully charged, called to Nikki and climbed onto my bed. Sitting there cross legged I pulled up Jake and hit message on my cell.

I waited and waited and waited. Nothing. Damn it, I knew it was too good to be true. I threw the phone on the bed and headed for the bathroom to take a shower.

As I reached for the faucet, I heard the phone beep.... message from Jake...

I ran for the bed and picked up the phone.

"Hi Gigi, how was your day? I thought about you and wondered if I would hear from you again."

"Yeah, I wondered if I was going to hear from you too. So, are you at work now?"

"No, not yet. Go in at ten thirty tonight. What are you doing right now?"

"I was fixing to get into the shower, but I heard there was a message from you, so I decided to read it first."

"What do you have on right now?"

Wow!!!! This guy is wasting no time is he...I said to Nikki.

"A t-shirt and a pair of cutoffs. Why?"

"Aww babe that is sooo sexy.... bet you look really cute."

"It's comfortable."

"How are you wearing your hair? Is it long or short?"

"It's long and I wear it down. Mousy brown."

"Nice. I bet you are a sexy little thing. Have you ever done sex on the phone or by text?"

"No. I've never even talked about sex with someone I don't know. Why are you asking me about this? I must be crazy to be doing this."

"You're not crazy Hun. We all need a release in one way or another. Why not this way? Try it... you might like it. If not, we will stop. You are in control, ok?"

Well, it seemed harmless enough. What could it hurt? "Nikki, what do you think? "She licked my hand as I petted her back as if to tell me it would be fine.

"Alright Jake, but you're going to have to help me with this as it's all new to me. So how do we begin?"

" :) Ok baby. .. relax...let whatever happens come naturally. We just start talking. What are you doing?"

"I'm lying on my bed texting you."

"Are you comfortable?"

"Yes."

"Have you ever played with your breasts?"

"Yeah."

"Okay, rub your breasts honey. Massage them, one at a time. Oh, how does that feel?"

"Feels good."

"You still have your t-shirt on?"

"Yes. Is that okay?"

"Oh yes baby...that is just fine. Pinch your nipples and get them hard honey."

"Ahh, yeah, that does feel good. What else do you want me to do?"

"Do you feel like you're getting wet?"

"Kinda."

"That's good. When you feel the need, put your hand down on your crotch and rub it. I bet that feels really good doesn't it sweetheart?"

"Yeah, but it's hard to do that and text you too."

"It's ok, you're doing just fine. How does your pussy feel honey?"

"Wet and hot and excited. She is so horny. Wow, I can't believe this feels so great."

"You like this huh...not so bad is it? You think you can get yourself off?"

"No problem there. How about you? What are you doing?"

"Baby, my cock is so hard just thinking of you playing with your pussy. I want to cum so bad."

"OMG, I'm going to cum....oh yeah I'm cummmmmming."

"Squeeze those titties and rub that pussy baby...make yourself cum....oh yeah girl, go with it Gigi...enjoy it."

"Oh yes...it was great. OMG...I can't believe I just did that. I can't believe it."

Gigi laid on her bed in stunned disbelief. What the hell had she just done? And why had she done this with a man she didn't know and by text on the phone? Was she that hard up? All kinds of thoughts were going rampantly through her mind.

"Gigi, are you there? Are you okay?" asked Jake.

OMG, I can't talk to him now...what can I say?

"Yes, I'm here".

"Well, how was that for your first experience in text phone sex? What do you think?"

"It was great. I've never done anything like this before and it was mind blowing. You are a very good teacher. Did you cum too?"

"Oh yea baby...I came a lot...I need to go clean up and go to work. Can I text you later?"

"I'm really kind of tired and I have to go into work early in the morning. How bout I text you after I get home in the evening?"

"Sure, whatever works best for you."

"Okay Jake, have a good night at work.... later."

After I hung up the phone I sat there and stared at the phone.

'What the hell am I doing? But I do feel so relaxed and sleepy. Come on Nikki, let's get some sleep."

The next morning Gigi showered and went into the kitchen to have her morning coffee. She didn't function without her caffeine. As she looked at the kitchen walls,she remembered her conversation with Jake the night before. What color should she paint them? That had led to the best climax she had had in weeks. Was this a fluke or could this lead into something fantastic? What else could Jake teach her about the joys of text sex? Hum....guess I'll have to wait until this evening to find out now won't I.

Where do Jake and Gigi take their new found relationship from here...

Follow Jake and Gigi's adventure in my next book: PASSIONS AND PLEASURES